Disney's

My Very First Winnie the Pooh™

Be Patient, Pooh

Kathleen W. Zoehfeld Illustrated by Robbin Cuddy

Disney
PRESS

NEW YORK

Printed in the United States of America.
Based on the Pooh Stories by A. A. Milne (copyright The Pooh Properties Trust).

FIRST EDITION
1 3 5 7 9 10 8 6 4 2

Library of Congress Catalog Card Number: 99-68125
ISBN: 0-7868-3250-9

For more Disney Press fun, visit www.disneybooks.com

Disney's

My Very First Winnie the Pooh

Be Patient, Pooh

One morning Winnie the Pooh woke up thinking about cake and presents and balloons. It's not every day that a bear wakes up thinking of cake and presents and balloons. But today was Pooh's birthday, and his friends were giving him a party.

A birthday party for me, thought Pooh excitedly. I can't wait!

He put on his slippers and shuffled over to his clock. "Is it time for my birthday party yet?" he asked. Pooh's clock didn't say anything. The little hand pointed quietly at the eight and the big hand pointed at twelve. Breakfast time, thought Pooh. That's always a good time.

He set out three pots of honey. "By the time I've finished these, it'll be almost time for my party," he said hopefully.

Pooh licked and licked. But when he'd licked the last drop of honey from the bottom of the last pot, it was still not time for his party.

Pooh did his stoutness exercises. Then he did his stoutness exercises again. But still, it was not time for his party.

"I'd better go to Rabbit's house to see how the party is coming along," decided Pooh. He hurried up the path.

"Everything's just fine," said Rabbit, standing at his door and blocking Pooh's view. "The party will be ready at supper time."

"Can I see my cake?" asked Pooh. He tried to look around Rabbit to find it.

"Not yet," said Rabbit. "Supper time!"

Pooh sighed. The day was not anywhere near
supper time yet. And the morning had already gone
on longer than any other morning he could remember.
He sat down on his favorite rock near the stream. He
watched the bubbly water racing past. "The water
must be rushing to a birthday party," sighed Pooh.

Maybe having a little company would help pass the time, thought Pooh.

He knocked at Piglet's door, and he heard the sound of paper rustling inside. "Are you wrapping my present, Piglet?" he asked.

"Don't come in yet!" cried Piglet. He finished tying a pink ribbon around Pooh's present and tucked it in the closet.

Then he called out, "You can come in now!"

"Can I see my present, Piglet? What do you think we'll do at the party, Piglet? Do you think Rabbit will put pink roses on my cake? How much longer do you think it'll be, Piglet?" asked Pooh all in a big jumble.

He settled in Piglet's comfy chair. "It is nice to have company to talk to about all these things," said Pooh. "It helps pass the time in a friendly way. Doesn't it?"

Piglet had opened his mouth and was trying to decide which question to answer first, when Tigger and Roo knocked at the door.

"Lunchtime!" cried Tigger as he and Roo bounced in.

Piglet looked at his clock. The big hand and the little hand were both pointing at twelve.

"Lunchtime," said Pooh thoughtfully. "That's a lot closer to supper time than breakfast time is, isn't it?"

"It's right NOW," said Tigger, who was quite hungry and had no idea which things were closer to what other things.

"Lunchtime is one of my favorite times of day," said Pooh. He helped Piglet and Tigger and Roo set the table.

As he was licking his last pot of honey clean, he sighed happily. "This is almost like a party right now."

"Oh, no," said Tigger, "a party has streamers and noisemakers and fancy hats and ice cream and . . . "

Pooh thought about streamers and noisemakers and fancy hats and ice cream (mmm, with plenty of honey) and cake and presents and balloons . . . "Is it almost time for the party?" he asked.

"Oh, d-dear, I hope not," said Piglet. "I promised to help Rabbit decorate."

"Me, too," said Tigger.

"Me, too, too," said Roo.

Piglet and Tigger and Roo hurried off to Rabbit's house.

Pooh decided to wash Piglet's lunch dishes. By the time I finish these, it will be time for my party, he thought. But when he had dried the last drop of water from the last dish, it was still not time for his party.

"Waiting is hard," sighed Pooh. "Maybe I should ask Christopher Robin if he knows something about it."

"Why does it take SO long for a party to come?" asked Pooh at Christopher Robin's door.

"It just SEEMS long, Pooh," said Christopher Robin. "When you have to wait, the best thing to do is something you really like."

"What do bears like to do?" asked Pooh, hoping Christopher Robin could remind him.

"Well, I'm reading this great story about a pirate bear who's looking for buried treasure," said Christopher Robin. "Would you like me to read it to you?"

"Oh, would you?" said Pooh happily.

They snuggled together under a shady tree, and Christopher Robin read and read. Pooh forgot all about cake and presents and balloons. He closed his eyes and saw tall ships, rolling waves, and buried treasure. They were just getting to "X marks the spot" when Christopher Robin thought he'd better check his watch.

The little hand pointed at the five, and the big hand pointed at twelve. "Supper time!" said Christopher Robin.

"You mean it's time for my party ALREADY?" cried Pooh.

Christopher Robin took Pooh's present from its hiding place and started off for Rabbit's house. "Come on, Pooh," he called.

"Cake and presents and balloons! It's time, it's time, it's time!" sang Pooh as they walked along together.

Pooh was the first one to reach the door. Rabbit swung it open and shouted, "Happy birthday!"

Inside, Pooh saw his beautiful birthday cake with pink roses, and honeypots all wrapped in crinkly paper, and lots of colorful balloons, and streamers, and all his friends in fancy hats shouting, "Happy birthday, Pooh!"

"Oh!" cried Pooh. "Party time is my favorite time ever!"

Then Pooh hugged his good friends Piglet and Christopher Robin.

"And thanks to you," he whispered, "waiting was a grand time, too."